A Whitman TWEEN-AGE Book

In-between books for in-between readers

DORY BOY

ABOUT THIS BOOK

Danny faced into the wind. He liked having the salt spray sting his eyes.

The sky was still gray-pink. The fog hugged the water. Chattering sea gulls were circling the pier looking for handouts. A few early-morning fishermen looked down at them from the pier and waved. And so began Danny's summer of work and fun.

Danny was to learn much about the sea—that it could, as old Jaywalk said, turn from friend to foe in a minute. He was to learn much about people—about old Max who was so unfriendly, and about George who spent his days in the surf. And he was to learn much about himself, about how he would act in the face of danger.

How Danny came through the challenges of that summer is the story told in DORY BOY.

DORY
BOY

by

JOAN
TALMAGE
WEISS

illustrated by

HOWARD
FORSBERG

WHITMAN PUBLISHING COMPANY • Racine, Wisconsin

CONTENTS

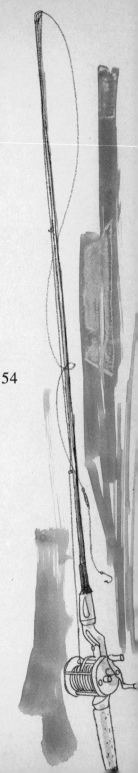

FIRST DAY OUT

"Hi, Dad," Danny said.

He had come out to the kitchen to eat breakfast, but he was still half asleep. It was four o'clock in the morning. Only dory fishermen and milkmen ate breakfast so early, Danny thought. He yawned. Why, it was so early even the flies were still asleep.

"Good morning, son," Dad said over his newspaper. "Are you ready for a big day?"

11

"Sure am," Danny said. He brushed back his blond hair and sat down at the table. He was tall for a ten-year-old.

Mom gave him a plate of eggs and bacon. "Eat up, Danny," she said. "A dory boy needs a good breakfast under his belt."

Danny grinned. He turned to Dad. "How's the surf this morning?"

"Well, the tide is high, which is bad," Dad said. "But the wind is low, which is good. We'll get our boat out through the waves all right."

Danny nodded. A high tide meant more water for their boat to cross. But the low wind meant that the water would be calm.

Danny started to eat. Today was the first day of summer vacation. And today was the first day Dad had asked him to be his dory boy. Other summers Danny had worked on the beach *selling* the fish. Today he was going to help *catch* the fish.

Danny wondered if the shivers he felt were from the cold or from his own excitement. Both were all mixed up together in this strange night time of morn-

12

ing. This was a strange time, a different time of day. And he felt a little strange himself.

"What time did Jim get going, Mom?" Danny asked.

Mom looked up. "Around three," she said. "The 'Princess' pulls out at five-thirty."

Jim was Danny's thirteen-year-old brother. Jim was crewing on a pleasure fishing boat this morning. All last year Jim had been Dad's dory boy. Now it was Danny's turn. And Danny wanted to do the very best job he could. He wanted Dad and Mom to be as proud of him as they were of Jim, and that was really asking something.

"I hope he likes working for those fishermen," Dad said. "It's a long ways from just him and me out at sea in the 'Gretchen.' "

Like most boats, their dory boat had a lady's name. Dad and Jim had thought long and hard before naming her "Gretchen." The name had eight letters in it. Fishermen believed that brought good luck.

The door opened and Nancy shuffled in. "Gee,

13

you're as noisy as Jim," she kidded Danny.

"All boys are noisy," Mom said. "Go back to sleep, sweetheart."

But Nancy was wide awake. "Daddy, can I go out on the dory? Please? Oh, *please,* Daddy?" She stood tall, on tiptoe, to look bigger than eight. "I'm not so little, Daddy."

Dad laughed. "You aren't little at all. But the dory boat is small. I'll say this: If you help Mom on the beach this summer, I'll take you out the day before school starts. Okay?"

Nancy jumped up and down. "Goody, goody," she cried. "Oh, I'll work hard, Daddy, and you don't have to pay me, either."

"Speaking of money—" Dad stood up. "Here's the money for baiting my hooks yesterday." He handed Danny a dollar.

"Gee, thanks, Dad," Danny said. "But you don't have to pay me—not until I'm good enough, that is."

"From now on I will," Dad said. "You'll be doing a man's job out at sea."

14

Carefully Danny folded the money. One whole dollar! He started for his room.

"What're you going to buy with all your money?" Nancy asked.

Danny stopped. He would save it. By the end of summer he would have quite a lot. And he knew what he wanted more than anything else.

"A bike," Danny said quickly. "I'll save for a ten-speed bike. Then I won't have to walk to school next year."

Dad laughed out loud. "What's the matter with a three-speed?" he asked.

"Well, Dad," Danny said, thinking fast. "You can go faster with a ten-speed."

Dad laughed. "That's my boy," he said. "If you're going to try for something, try for the very best."

Mom was smiling, too, but Nancy just giggled. "Show-off," she whispered.

Danny started to take a poke at her. But he stopped because Mom and Dad were watching.

"Okay, little girl," he said. "You'd better be on

the beach today when Dad and I come in. No goofing off this summer."

Nancy made a face, but Mom said, "We'll be there. It looks like a good clear day."

Dad stepped outside and looked up at the sky. "It's a good fish-selling day," he said. "Where's my lucky hat?"

Danny handed him his old straw hat with all the silly feathers and fishhooks on it. All the dorymen kidded Dad about his hat. But he always wore it— for luck.

A fisherman needed only two things to make good. He needed luck and timing. That's what Jaywalk, one of the dorymen, had often told Danny. Luck was there or it wasn't. But timing was knowing when to push out through the waves and where to catch the most fish. Timing came from inside the doryman himself.

Danny jabbed his arms into his Windbreaker jacket and shoved his feet into long, black, waterproof boots.

Mom handed him something. It was a lemon.

17

"In case you need it." She spoke so low Nancy and Dad couldn't hear her.

"But I won't need it," Danny said firmly. He didn't want Mom's old seasick cure.

Mom had the same blue eyes Danny had. And now she looked into his eyes hard. "I know you won't, Danny. It's just nice to have." Then she added, "Jim always carries one. It will be a secret between Jim and you and me."

Danny shrugged. He took the lemon and pushed it down deep into his pocket. Well, he thought, nobody had to *know* about it except him and Mom.

Danny climbed into the white pickup truck beside Dad. It was still dark outside. Dad drove with his headlights on.

There were no other cars on the street, so they got to the beach beside the pier in just five minutes. Dad stepped out and took in a deep breath of salt air.

"This is the nicest time of day, Danny," Dad said. "Quiet, fresh air, no people . . . it sure beats being a carpenter."

20

Danny said softly, "I know." He did understand. A couple of years ago Dad had hurt one hand in an accident when he was a carpenter. He could no longer handle a carpenter's tools very well, but he could fish with the hand. That was why Dad had bought the "Gretchen." The whole family had been fishing ever since.

Danny walked down the boardwalk with Dad to their locker. During the day the dory boats were turned into two rows of fish shops. Customers tramped down the boardwalk. They stared at—and sometimes bought—the fish.

But now it was pitch dark, and cold without the sun. Everything was very still and quiet. All Danny heard were the waves a half block down the beach. Some dory boats had already gone out fishing. But others still stood alone and empty, waiting for their owners.

"It looks as if the surfers beat us down here again," Dad chuckled. He unlocked their locker.

Danny looked through the pilings to the other side of the pier. Two fire circles blazed against the black

sky. Danny could see the surfers warming their hands in front of the fires. Their surfboards were still on the two-wheeled trailers hitched behind their bikes.

"I don't see George," Danny said. His friend spent every day, all day, riding the waves on top of his surfboard.

They began loading the "Gretchen." She was sea-tight and fourteen feet long. "Gretchen" was painted a sparkling white with black trim. She had an inside of orange-red. As Dad said, nobody ever missed "Gretchen" in the fog.

Danny heard an outboard motor fire up down by the waves. He knew that Max was already pushing out. Max was the doryman everybody was afraid of —everybody except Dad and old Jaywalk.

Just then Jaywalk came strolling up the board-walk toward them.

"Hi ya, boy," he called. "Are you ready for the big day?"

Danny grinned. Jaywalk was a real character. Mrs. Jaywalk, his wife, said he'd always been called

24

Jaywalk because he never did anything in a straight line. And he always got away with it.

"Sure, and I'm even going to get paid," Danny told him proudly.

"Just don't forget what I told you," Jaywalk said. "Always keep an eye on Mother Sea. She can turn on you quick as a minute."

"Yeah, yeah," Danny said. "Like you tell me, 'She's as fickle as a hurricane, but men couldn't live without her.'" Danny fixed the compass near the center seat.

"Many people would starve without her fish," Jaywalk said.

Dad crab walked up carrying the heavy outboard motor. Jaywalk helped him ease it over the back of the boat and chain it to the stern.

"Are you preaching at my kid again, Jaywalk?" Dad asked.

"Not preaching, James Allen," Jaywalk chuckled. "Teaching, yes. But preaching, no."

"Okay, okay," Dad had to laugh. "Are you going out today?"

"Sure am. I'm all set to go, but I'll give you a push first."

Dad smiled his thanks. They pushed the dory up onto the wooden rollers. Then all three of them began pushing "Gretchen" down the boardwalk toward the waves.

The sky was turning light, but the pier lights were still on. Danny listened to the waves. In the daytime he heard the soft words the waves whispered. Words like "In and out, in and out," or sometimes silly words like "Fresh fish, fresh fish for sale." But now he was too excited to listen quietly.

"Max just left," Jaywalk told Dad. "He plans to beat you back and get first spot."

"But if I'm first in, I'll get the first spot," Dad said.

The first spot was the best place in the double line of fish shops. That boat always sold out its catch by evening. But a boat at the end of the rows often had to sell to the fish cannery and not make as much money. The doryman who got that first spot was the first boat to come around the pier. The trouble was

Max liked to race Dad and then argue about the first spot.

"Dad," Danny asked, "why do you tell us kids to stay away from Max?"

"He's got his troubles, son," Dad said. "Lots of troubles."

"Yeah, and they are all inside of him," Jaywalk finished.

Danny wasn't sure he understood, but they had reached the waves. "Gretchen" was pointing bow first into the wind coming off the sea.

Dad and Jaywalk stood watching the waves break. They were timing the waves, first high ones, then low ones. Danny fingered the lemon in his pocket and was glad he had it.

At last the waves rolled in low and gentle. Now they had to move fast. This was the most dangerous time for a dory boat. The current could take a little dory boat and smash it against the pier before you could stop it.

"Okay, jump into the boat, Danny," Dad said. "Quick, now."

27

Danny got in and fit the oars into their locks. The two men pushed the boat into the water. When Dad climbed in, Jaywalk gave them one big push and let go.

"Good fishing," Jaywalk called. "Don't catch my pickup truck out there."

Danny giggled. Once Jaywalk had pulled up the tail gate of a pickup truck on his line. Ever since, he had bragged that he was going to catch the rest of the truck!

"We'll leave that for you," Dad called back as he leaned against the oars.

Now they needed both luck and timing. Danny sat still in the stern beside the outboard motor. He waited for Dad's order.

"The current is strong," Dad muttered. "That motor had better start up or. . . ."

Danny held his breath and waited. When the oars didn't touch bottom, Dad called, "Okay, pull the rope."

29

Danny pulled. The motor didn't start. He pulled again, harder. Still nothing. The current had turned the boat sideways. She was heading straight for the pier. Jaywalk was yelling something to him from the shore.

"Here, let *me*." Dad changed places with Danny. He gave the rope a hard pull. The motor sputtered and then started.

Quickly Dad swung the boat away from the pier. They hit a few waves straight on. But they both grinned. Everything was all right now.

Danny took a deep breath and asked, "Where are we going, Dad?"

"Four miles straight off the pier," Dad said. "I got lots of sea trout there yesterday."

Danny turned and faced into the wind. He liked having the salt spray sting his eyes.

The sky was still gray-pink. The fog hugged the water. Chattering sea gulls were circling the pier looking for handouts. A few early-morning fishermen looked down at them from the pier and waved. Danny waved back.

First Day Out

They rounded the pier and pointed straight out to sea. Danny felt the hum of the motor through his boots. He leaned forward and tried to see what lay ahead.

It was all sea water—miles and miles of nothing but salt water. He was full of the love of the sea and the fear of being seasick.

TROUBLE WITH MAX

Dad ran the boat straight out to sea. He looked back to see if he was in line with the pier. Also, he watched the compass to be sure he was straight on course.

Danny swallowed hard. He still didn't know if he was seasick or just excited. He felt all mixed up inside.

Quickly he took a bite from his lemon. Then he ate it—all but the skin. Mom was right, he thought. It was a nice thing to have. He felt a little better already.

After a while Dad moved the motor lever to low speed and stood up. They were out at sea.

"Time to throw the hooks, Danny," he said. "Give me a hand here, now."

Danny helped Dad move the big wooden tub of fishing line up on top of the center seat. Then, with a big splash, Dad threw the anchor overboard.

"Here she goes," he said, tipping the tub over the side. With a zip, the baited hooks on the long line unwound from the bottom of the tub. The moving boat spread the line out straight. But it was the anchor that pulled the line to the bottom of the sea.

"Boy, that was fast." Danny was amazed. All the hooks were set and Dad put down the wooden tub. Then he fastened the end of the fishing line to a black marker float and threw it overboard.

Dad hummed while he worked, and Danny be-

33

gan to enjoy himself. Dad baited his two trolling lines.

"When do we pull up the line?" Danny asked. He kept watching the black marker bobbing in the water.

"Oh, in an hour or so," Dad said. "Okay, Danny, take the motor."

They changed places. Danny shot the boat away from the line. This was his biggest job, so he wanted

to run the boat smoothly for Dad. Dad dropped both trolling lines over the side.

Slowly they began to drag the two fishing lines in the water. They were trolling for bonito. The hooks bobbed along behind the boat, skipping on top of the water. Danny smiled. They looked as if they were dancing.

"How come bonito only bite on a trolling line?" Danny had to know. There was so very much to learn!

"They are like the tuna," Dad explained. "Bonito only strike at moving bait."

Danny trolled slowly around and around in a very wide circle. All at once one line snapped tight. Dad pulled it in. There on the hook flapped a graceful bonito.

"Gee, he's a big one," Danny said, leaning over the rail. "Look at him fight, Dad."

"Yeah, they're awfully fast in the water," Dad agreed.

Dad brought in the fish, cut it, and flipped it into the bow. Danny looked at the shiny blue and green lines on the fish. Nothing was as colorful as a bonito right out of the sea.

Humming, Dad baited the hook again and threw it over the side. Danny never changed the speed of the boat—that way Dad caught more fish.

They circled around and around for an hour. Slowly the bow filled up with fish. Danny watched while he kept the boat at the same slow speed. Dad was very fast. When a bonito swallowed the hook, Dad worked it out with sharp-pointed pliers.

"Gotta be careful of these," Dad said. "They have teeth like tiny needles."

"Jaywalk said they can even bite through your fingernail," Danny said.

"That's right," Dad chuckled. "I've got the marks to prove it."

Danny felt something warm on his back. He turned around to see that the sun had come out. The fog began to lift off the water.

"Blue water today," Dad said.

"What does that mean?" Danny asked.

"Blue water means sharks. Green water means bonito. We'd better get back to our line and see what's going on there."

Dad pulled in the trolling lines. Then they went searching for their marker.

Danny had been so busy trolling and watching Dad fish that he hadn't looked around. But now he looked out across the sea. He looked in all four

37

directions. No matter which way he looked, all he saw was water. There wasn't a boat anywhere. They were alone on the huge sea. It gave Danny the feeling that they were the only people in the whole world.

"Good thing we have the compass, Dad," Danny yelled above the motor.

Dad nodded. "It's an awfully big ocean to find one small black flag," he called back.

He saw the marker before Danny did. He pointed and Danny saw it bobbing in the water. Danny laughed. The black flag was flapping like mad in the wind.

Danny pulled up alongside and cut the motor. Dad let the boat drift while he pulled on a pair of thick gloves. Then he picked up the marker and began winding up the fishing line on the winch. First he wound with one hand, then he wound with the other. It took a long time to wind in all the line from the bottom.

"Can I help, Dad?" Danny asked. The rocking of the boat was pitching him all over the place.

"Move the tub over to the side," Dad said.

Glad to be busy, Danny shoved the tub into place. Looking down into the water he saw the first hook coming up. It had something on it.

"Hey, Dad, you caught some kind of a monster," Danny yelled.

Dad stopped cranking and came over. "Oh, that's a slimy eel," he said with a frown. "They're nasty things."

"Can you eat them?" Danny had to know.

"Not this kind. But scientists use them to study. They have three hearts. If you cut them in three pieces each piece will live."

"How neat." Danny was amazed that such an ugly thing could be so clever.

Dad cut the eel off the hook with his knife and threw it back. He put the tub between his knees. Then he began to pull up the line, hand over hand.

Danny watched eagerly.

First a sea trout came up. Flip! Off it went into the tub. Next came a red rock cod.

"Look at Popeye," Danny called out. That was what some customers called rock cod. The red fish

40

always came up with eyes bulging and tongue out. That was because they were deepwater fish, used to the great pressure down below.

"Can I pull up one?" Danny asked eagerly.

"You can try," Dad said with a funny smile.

Excitedly Danny pulled on a pair of gloves and stood beside Dad. Slowly Dad passed the line into his hands. Pow! The weight almost pulled Danny overboard. Dad grabbed the line back.

"Gosh!" Danny breathed easier.

"It's like pulling up the bottom of the sea," Dad said with a chuckle. "Can't you just see old Jaywalk pulling up that tail gate?"

"It must have been awfully heavy," Danny agreed. He wouldn't try that again until he was older.

Together they looked down into the water. The water was so clear they could see the line coming up with the fish on it.

Danny began to call out, "I see a sea trout, another sea trout, a rock cod. Oh, oh, what's that?"

"That's a shark." Dad pulled it up. "He's all wrapped up like a Christmas package."

42

Danny stared. Sure enough, the shark had fought so hard he had twisted himself up in the line. What a mess! "What kind is he, Dad?" Danny couldn't stop looking at that large, ugly mouth.

"This is a pin-back shark," said Dad, working at the snarled line. "But he's not a keeper."

Dad cut off the shark's tail so he wouldn't steal fish again. Then he threw him back in. Dad was fast with the knife. "There's nothing worse than to look down and see your line full of sharks," Dad went on. "Remember last summer when Jim and I came back with only ten bonito?"

Danny nodded, then went back to calling out the fish as they came up. "Sea trout, rock cod, another eel—ugh, how slimy! Hey, look! Here comes another shark. . . ."

Some sharks Dad kept because customers liked them. Others he had to throw back.

"Say, Danny, why don't you throw a line in the water?" Dad said. "Maybe you'll catch a whale. You never can tell."

"Who wants a whale? I'd like a ling cod."

Danny baited his hook. Last summer Jim had caught a ling cod on a rod and reel. It had been so heavy Jim could hardly carry it. It weighed in at thirty-one pounds—the heaviest ling cod the dory fleet had ever caught. Boy, had that fish made Jim famous! He had even got his picture in the newspaper.

Carefully Danny cast his line out into the water. "Come on," he thought. "Look sharp, you big feeders out there."

Waiting for a bite, Danny found himself humming along with Dad.

"Well, I'll be," Dad said. "A starfish—nice and lilac."

Danny had to go look. "Hey, let's take that back to Mom," Danny said. "She'll like the color."

"It'll lose the color," Dad said, "unless you water it down all the way back."

Danny agreed. "I'll keep it watered," he said, and put the starfish up in the bow. This was sure a lot of fun out here.

Danny wondered about Jim on the "Princess."

Did he like crewing on a pleasure fishing boat? Or was working on a dory boat better?

Danny was used to the rocking of the boat now. He found he could even stand up and roll with the boat while he fished.

"I guess your ling cod has already had breakfast," Dad kidded him.

"Maybe," Danny said slowly. Just then he felt a jerk on his line. He started reeling in, but the hook was empty.

"You jerked it out of his mouth," Dad told him. "Don't be in such a hurry."

Danny blushed and baited his hook. But this time he ran the hook through the bait twice for luck.

Almost at the same time the hook hit the water, a bonito struck. The fish almost pulled the rod out of Danny's hands.

"Let him run with it," Dad yelled. "Let him get good and tired."

Danny let the line spin off the reel. His heart was beating somewhere around his throat. Boy, a fish of his own. . . .

45

"Okay, now reel in fast," Dad said. "Don't let him horse you."

Danny reeled in. The fish zigzagged through the water, trying to get away. The pull was fierce, but Danny never stopped reeling. Finally he had his fish right up to the boat. Dad reached over with his gaff and brought the fish in.

"Good work, son," he said. "You caught yourself a fine bonito."

Proudly Danny looked down at his fish. But somehow it looked smaller out of the water. Still, it was his very first fish. "Can we eat him for dinner?" he asked eagerly.

"Let's ask your mother," Dad said. "Here comes the anchor, so we can go back in."

Dad's watch said nine o'clock. Danny was surprised. Had they really been out at sea four whole hours? It seemed like a few minutes.

Dad headed the boat back toward land. Danny went back to his work. First he moved all the fish from the bow to the tub. Then he started wiping down the boat with a wet sponge. A clean boat drew more customers on the beach.

The fog was gone and the sky was blue. A sailboat drifted off at the horizon. How little it looked, Danny thought. It didn't seem far away. Instead it looked like a toy sailboat. And it was the only boat they had seen all morning.

Dad stood up and pointed. "Look ahead. Over that way."

Danny stood up. Something brown was floating in the water. "What is it?" he yelled. "Logs?"

"More like dogs," Dad chuckled. "Those are two seals taking a sunbath."

Danny giggled. "A sunbath in the water," he repeated.

Slowly Dad nosed the boat toward the floating animals. Sure enough, two seals lay on their backs in the water. They had their heads back, eyes closed, and their flippers up in the warm sun. They were so close Danny could see their whiskers.

"Hey there, silly," Danny called out. He couldn't stop laughing.

One seal opened his eyes and saw them. Right

away he rolled over and dove under the sea. The other seal watched them, then dove, too. Then both seals began to play in the water. First they came up, turned over, and fell backward into the water. Then they dove out of sight and came up all around the boat. They looked as if they were grinning from ear to ear.

"Boy, look at them laugh!" Danny said. "Don't they have a blast?"

Dad nodded. "They are born clowns. And they really put on a show, don't they?" Then he added, "Well, Danny, we'd better get back to shore. Mother will be waiting."

He turned up the motor and the boat shot forward. But Danny watched the seals until they were out of sight.

When Danny turned around he saw that Max's boat was coming in, too. But they were a little ahead of him. Max looked up, frowned, and pushed his motor up to full speed. The two boats raced to shore. Danny felt the "Gretchen" hit the soft sand of the beach.

It was almost a tie. But Danny knew that they had come around the pier first. Their boat should have first spot on the boardwalk.

Max jumped out into the shallow waves. He shoved his boat onto the sand. "You lost today, James Allen," he called out.

Dad jumped out of the "Gretchen," his face set. Danny could tell he was mad. "I don't want to fight again, Max," he said very slowly. "But we were first around the pier."

The sound of his voice shot a ripple of fear down Danny's back. He looked up the boardwalk to Mom and Nancy coming down to meet them. Jaywalk was running his boat in to shore fast. But he was standing up, watching the trouble. Ed, the handyman on the beach, was coming down to help with the boats.

Danny looked from Dad to Max and back again. Neither would give in. Now what would happen? he wondered.

S.O.S. DORY BOAT TURNED OVER

Jaywalk was the first to reach them. He jumped into the water and steadied his dory with both hands. "What's the trouble here?" he asked.

"Same old story," Dad shrugged.

"I was first in," Max said in a loud voice. "But *he* wants first spot again."

Jaywalk snorted angrily. "Now, look here," he said slowly. "I was watching you both. James Allen was the first around the pier."

54

Max didn't say anything. He didn't even look toward Mom and Nancy when they hurried up.

"What happened?" Nancy whispered. "He looks awful mad."

Danny told her quickly. Then they both looked at Dad to see what was going to happen.

But it was Jaywalk who said, "Come on, kids. Get the rollers. We'll push up the 'Gretchen' first."

Danny and Nancy ran to get the wooden rollers, so they didn't hear what Max was mumbling.

Ed was ready to help. He kept the beach clean for the dorymen and did odd jobs. They all pushed "Gretchen" up onto the rollers. Then they began to push her along the beach over the boardwalk.

First the boat rolled over a roller. Then Danny grabbed the rope handle and dragged the roller up to the bow. Then they were ready to push again.

"Let's make this dory boat fly," Jaywalk called out.

Nancy and Danny pushed right along with the men. By their pushing together at the same time, the boat moved up the beach easily. Danny could

see customers standing at the top of the boardwalk. They were waiting to buy fish.

Everything went fast now. Mom got the knives, sieve, and washing pans out of their locker. She unrolled the clean white paper from around them.

The "Gretchen" sat in the first spot alongside the boardwalk. Danny began shoveling a hole in the sand for the oar. He buried the blade end so that the oar made a post. Then Nancy hung the weighing scales from the top.

Dad carried the outboard motor to the locker and brought back the cutting board. It fit neatly over the stern of the dory.

"Turn on the water, Danny," Dad called.

Danny got the hose and turned on the water. Dad washed down the boat carefully. Their fish were food and had to be kept very clean.

While they worked, Nancy asked, "How was it out there? Fun?"

Danny shrugged. "Well, it was all right." But his grin admitted it was more than that.

"I can hardly wait for the last day of vacation,"

57

Nancy said. "I get to go out with you."

"It's really neat," Danny told her.

Mom put the display rack on the middle seat of the dory. Then she began gaffing the fish and laying them in neat rows inside the display rack. The gaff was a thick stick with a sharp hook on the end.

Dad put up their big green umbrella so that it shaded the boat. Jaywalk was the only doryman who had an umbrella with a flowered top. But then that was just like old Jaywalk, Danny thought—always different.

At the cutting board Danny began to sharpen the knives on the whetstone. The boat was now a fish shop and the waiting customers began to crowd in around it.

"I want those red ones," a man said quickly.

Mom gaffed the rock cod and slapped them into the weighing scales. "That's a dollar fifteen," she said.

The man nodded.

"How much for the sea trout?" a lady asked.

"Thirty cents a pound," Dad said.

60

"Hey, Mommy," a little boy said. "Look at all the fishies."

Dad moved the sold fish to the cutting board. While his customers watched, Danny began to clean and scale the fish. Nancy stood next to him, ready with the wash pans.

"Do you want these filleted, sir?" Danny asked. Filleting meant more work, since the backbone had to be cut out and the fish skinned. But then, they charged more for fillets.

"No, leave them whole," the man said, getting out his money.

As soon as Danny cleaned the fish, Nancy washed them. Mom wrapped them up in a newspaper. Then she took a rubber band from an abalone shell and snapped it around the package. Last she collected the man's money.

It wasn't much past nine o'clock in the morning, and they were already selling fish.

"I sure hope we have a good day," Danny said in a low voice to Nancy.

"Me, too," she said.

61

They looked up to see Jaywalk, Ed, and Max push in Max's boat. Max's boat took second spot, but he didn't look happy. Everybody left him alone.

A pair of bare feet stopped beside Danny and somebody said, "Hi, sport." It was George, who was a big, tall twelve-year-old. He was wearing his black rubber shirt, and his swim trunks were wet. He had been out on his surfboard already this morning, early though it was.

"Hi, George," Danny said, keeping on with his work. "How's the surf?"

"Flat as a bowl of soup," George said sadly. "I'm waiting for high tide and those big waves to ride. Hey, Danny, can I borrow a dollar?" George was as bad as the sea gulls—always looking for a hand-out.

Dad heard him and came up. "There are some hooks to be baited over there." He pointed to their wooden bucket standing on a low locker.

George laughed. "Okay. How much?"

"Just what I pay Danny here," Dad said. "One dollar."

"It's a deal." George shot Danny a wink and went to work.

Nancy got tired working so Dad sent her across the street to get him hot coffee. The sun was out but a cold wind still blew. Dad took over the fish cleaning and Danny did the washing.

Mom stood beside the display case and asked customers, "Would you folks like a fish today?" Many people stopped, and some bought.

The rock cod sold out first. Then the sea trout and bonito began to sell, but more slowly. Lots of people crowded around to watch. Danny could feel all those eyes staring and staring. Would he ever get used to it? he wondered.

He looked up from his work. "Hey, Mom," he called. "I caught that one bonito there myself." He pointed it out. "Can we . . . I was wondering . . . do you suppose we can have him for dinner tonight, Mom?"

"If this is your first fish, Danny, we'll eat him," Mom said.

Danny flushed because some customers had over-

heard them. But still Mom had agreed. He went to show her the lilac starfish, but Dad was right. The animal had changed to a dull sandy color. So Danny gave him to a little boy whose mother was buying a fish.

"Hey, thanks a lot," the little boy said.

Danny smiled. "You're welcome." He could tell it was the boy's first starfish. And Danny remembered how·exciting that feeling was.

More dory boats came in until there were two rows of boats along the boardwalk. Business was steady for a long time. Then Danny had time to drink the hot chocolate Nancy brought him. It tasted great.

The sun was getting warmer all the time. Danny took off his jacket. He sat up on top of the locker where George was still baiting hooks and watched him work.

The little kids were feeding graham crackers to the red ants who lived in the sand. Some of them were playing hide-and-seek in and around the empty dory boats.

"Be sure to bait the hook twice," Danny told George.

George looked up. "I don't get it," George said. "Do you mean that I should put *two* fish on each hook?"

"No." Danny showed him how to push the hook once through the salted anchovy. Then he showed him how to turn the hook and push it through the bait again. "Now it'll hold when the line hits the water," Danny explained.

"Boy, what a drag," George grumbled, but he looked at Danny carefully. "How about going surfing when I'm finished? You can borrow my board if you want to."

68

Danny nodded. "That would be great—if Dad doesn't need me."

Danny studied the surf. The tide had come in, and the waves were building up into higher and higher crests.

"The surf's up," he told George. That was the surfer's way of saying the waves were high enough to carry a surfer and his board all the way in to shore.

George grinned. "Let me out of here," he said, and worked faster.

Danny jumped down from his seat on the locker and helped George. He wound the fishing line around the inside of the wooden bucket. He laid each baitfish neatly against the side. The work went faster and soon George was finished.

"Thanks, sport," George said. "I'll buy you a malt."

"It's a deal." Danny never turned down an offer of food.

Dad handed George a dollar after looking over the bait job. "Looks like Danny's work," he said with a knowing grin.

"It was," George said sheepishly. "Well, part of it anyway."

"Say, Dad," Danny asked quickly. "Can I take a quick swim?"

They looked around. The customers had thinned out. Nancy was back washing fish. Mom was standing beside the display rack.

"Okay, Danny," Dad said. "But be back in an hour."

Both George and Danny grinned. Then they heard Max say, "I'm going out at three o'clock tomorrow morning so *nobody* can steal my first spot."

They all turned around. Max was talking to a customer, but he was looking at them.

Dad turned away quickly. "Go ahead, boys. Have fun."

George and Danny left. On the other side of the pier Danny took off his clothes. He had his swim trunks underneath. The sun felt warm on his bare back.

"Man, look at those combers!" George yelled, grabbing up his board.

70

The boys raced into the sea. George flopped down on top of his surfboard and began paddling. Danny threw himself into the first wave and began swimming. Soon they were out where the waves start, far from shore.

This was the best part about surfing. A good surfer knew how to watch the waves. He could tell when he could ride one in to shore.

George was a good surfer. Danny watched him carefully.

First George knelt on top of his board, waiting for a wave. When a big one started up, George paddled fast to move in front of it. Just as the wave began to break, George stood up on his board. He caught the wave just right. Then he went sailing in to shore balancing easily on the board, the wave breaking just behind him.

It was hard to do, Danny knew. But when you did everything right, it was the most exciting ride in the world.

After George rode a few waves, he turned his board over to Danny. After a couple of spills, Danny caught a wave just right. Faster and faster he sailed in to shore. What a thrill! This was as exciting as running the dory boat for the first time.

When he reached shore Danny looked toward the dory fleet. He saw many customers circled around the "Gretchen." He waved to George and floated the board out to him. Then, grabbing up his towel and clothes, he ran back to the boardwalk.

Danny had his shirt on when he reached the cutting board.

"Glad to see you," Dad said, working fast. "That man wants two sea trout."

Danny nodded, picked up the gaff, and weighed the fish. "Five pounds, sir," he told the man. "At thirty cents a pound that makes . . . ah. . . ." He tried to figure fast, but his mind seemed to stop and go blank.

The man smiled. "A dollar and a half," he said. "That will be fine."

Danny blushed and told himself that he would have to be faster next time.

But Dad said in a low voice, "You're doing fine, Danny." And then he felt better.

At the end of the day they had sold all but a few sea trout. Dad took those up to sell to the fish market. On his way he stopped, pulled out his wallet, and handed Danny a dollar.

"Awfully tired?" Dad asked.

"Not really." But Danny couldn't fool Dad. Danny was so tired that even his fingers ached.

"You should be," Mom said. "You've put in a man's day."

But Danny had one last chore. He loaded the wheelbarrow with their fish scraps and rolled it down the pier. At the very end he dumped the load into the sea. "That will bring in the seals," he thought.

When Danny got back Jim was there. His older brother looked sunburned but happy. "How did it go?" Jim asked him.

"Swell," Danny said. "How did you make out?"

"Ten dollars," Jim said proudly. He showed Danny the handful of paper money. "All of us bait boys split up the tips."

Danny's eyes almost popped. "Neat," he said slowly. Then he was so tired he could only wonder one thing over and over. Would he *ever* be as good a fisherman as Jim?

The next morning Danny went out with Dad again. They brought in a very good catch. They made first spot again. But the day after that, Max came in first, got first spot—and still he was mad. Dad and Jaywalk always helped to push his boat. But Max grumbled when they asked him to push theirs.

"Let's just leave him alone, Danny," Dad said again.

Summer had arrived. Lots of customers came to the beach every day. Most of the dory boats went out every day. This was their best time of year for fishing.

And every night Danny put another dollar in the handkerchief under his pillow. Boy, did those dollar bills ever crackle!

A month went by. Then another month. The high waves of summer had begun.

One morning Dad and Danny left a little late. They had to be extra careful pushing off through the surf. Sometimes the waves built up to seven feet high. But once they got out, the work went smoothly.

Dad had just set the lines when Danny heard a noise. Flap. Flap. A funny little bird flew up and landed on their dory.

Danny reached out. "Hey, Dad, what kind of bird is he?"

76

"I don't know," Dad said. "But he can't take off and fly unless he's on water. That silly bird has just stranded himself by landing on our boat."

"Then I'll keep him for a pet," Danny said excitedly. "Here, bird. Here, Gink."

Dad laughed. "What's a gink?" he asked.

"I don't really know," Danny said. "But he *looks* like a gink. Here, Gink."

The little gray bird waddled over. But he wouldn't let Danny touch him. He just stepped around, watching Danny with his little black eyes.

"Wonder of wonders," Danny thought. "We are all alone out here. We seldom even see another boat. But here comes a silly little bird."

Danny washed the salt off a baitfish and offered it to Gink. Snap. Gink took it right out of his hand.

When they started to troll, Danny said, "Hang on, Gink."

And Gink hung on. He couldn't take off and fly, so his little claws clamped onto the spray railing. Danny began making wide circles with the boat while Dad trolled the two lines.

All of a sudden they looked up. The big Coast Guard ship was coming toward them.

"Cut the motor, Danny," Dad yelled. "They want us."

Danny stopped the motor and the dory drifted. The huge Coast Guard ship came up alongside. All the men aboard were wearing their uniforms.

"Got some trouble up the beach," the Captain
called. "A dory boat is turned over in the waves."

Dad stood up, stiff and tense. "Is the doryman all
right?" Dad called back.

"Two lifeguards pulled him out," the Captain said.
"But our ship is too big to go into the waves. Can
you give us a hand with his dory?"

Dad didn't stop to think one minute. "Let's go,"

he called. Quickly he pulled in his trolling lines. "We'll follow you."

The Captain nodded and the big ship roared off.

"But, Dad," Danny asked, "what about our fishing line?"

"It'll have to wait," Dad said quickly. "Here, Danny, let me take the motor."

They changed places. Dad shot the motor up to top speed. Still it was hard to keep up with the big ship.

Danny looked at his new pet, teetering on the rail.

"Hang on, Gink," Danny whispered.

Gink held on for all he was worth.

Danny could feel a funny coldness creeping up inside of him. He was scared. Sure. But more than scared. Worried, too. What if it was old Jaywalk? After all his years of fishing?

"Who do you think it is?" Danny called back to Dad.

"It could be anybody," Dad's face was set. "Remember how rough it was this morning? Once a dory is caught in those waves. . . ."

80

Danny leaned forward to see better. The Coast Guard ship led them to a beach miles from their dory beach. Danny finally saw the little dory turned over in the waves. It was really helpless. The surging water was beating it against the sand.

It was an awful sight. All the gear was floating around in the water. One oar had even drifted out to sea.

Dad swung their boat and picked up the oar. He looked it over carefully.

"It's Max," he finally said.

"Now what do we do?" Danny asked.

"Go in and help him."

"But, Dad, our line—"

Dad shook his head. "Dorymen stick together, son."

That was all he said before he shot the "Gretchen" into the churning waves.

FINDING SECRET PAPERS

Instantly the rushing water circled their boat. The salt spray slapped Danny right in the face. He hunched down into his jacket and looked back at Dad, waiting for orders.

"Steady us with the oars," Dad yelled above the roar.

Danny obeyed, but the boat still rocked wildly.

83

Dad was already tying a line onto Max's boat. He was going to tow it to shore. But Max's boat had by this time turned right side up. Now it was full of water. That made it very heavy to pull along behind them.

Danny had to grab the rail to steady himself. He was already soaking wet. And the "Gretchen" was in the very same sea that had swamped Max's boat. What if *they* turned over, too?

Dad had both arms in the water. But he got the rope tied to Max's boat. When he straightened up he looked down at his wristwatch and made a face. It was ruined by the salt water. But Dad didn't stop. Never mind the watch. He turned to the motor and cranked it hard.

Danny saw that the Coast Guard ship was standing by out in deeper water. They couldn't come in closer without going aground, too. It was all up to Dad and the "Gretchen."

"I'm going to make a run for shore, Danny," Dad called through the flying spray. He took off his lucky hat and put it safely under the seat. Danny understood. It was better to take the hat off than risk losing it.

Danny turned around and looked at Gink. The poor little bird was scared stiff. His little black eyes were big and staring. He hung onto the railing, see-sawing this way and that with the roll of the boat. Danny knew he should let Gink go.

But he bit his lip. He didn't *want* to give up Gink. Gink was his new pet, and Nancy would love to have him waddling around the dory beach. They could feed him fish scraps. They could teach him to do tricks. They could. . . .

Gently Danny lowered Gink into the water. Instantly his wings began to beat. He took off in a straight line out to sea. Gink was leaving, but Danny couldn't watch. Their boat was in danger of swamping.

"Bail, Danny. Bail!" Dad yelled.

Danny set aside the oars and grabbed up a tin can. The water was ankle-deep inside the boat. He dipped up a full can of water and threw it overboard. Then another can. And another.

85

They moved toward shore. It was very slow going. Danny was tired and wanted to stop bailing. But he couldn't stop—not even to breathe.

He didn't look up from bailing until he felt the boat hit the beach. The two lifeguards waded out to meet them. They steadied the "Gretchen" while Dad jumped into the water and began pulling in Max's boat.

"Are you all right, Danny?" Dad asked.

Danny nodded. "I . . . I guess so."

It took all three men to get the water-filled boat in to shore. Danny could see Max standing on the shore—his arms at his sides, his face blank and staring. He didn't even move when they dragged his boat up onto the sandy beach. He just stared without seeing.

The lifeguards turned Max's boat over and drained out all the water. Dad waded back out to the "Gretchen." Danny had jammed both oars into the soft sand to hold her secure.

"Good work, Danny," Dad said. He looked tired, and tiny rivers of water ran down his face. Together

they pushed the "Gretchen" in to shore.

"Aren't we going back out?" Danny asked. He felt funny and numb all over. But still he couldn't forget one thing—they had left their fishing line out at sea.

"Not through those waves," Dad muttered. "They're killers."

The Coast Guard ship honked its horn. Dad waved them away. Everything was all right now.

Just then Danny saw Jaywalk backing a boat trailer down the beach toward them. His old truck had sand tires on it so it couldn't get stuck in the loose sand. Danny felt better.

"Here comes old Jaywalk," he told Dad.

"Just in the nick of time." Dad straightened, and a little smile showed around his mouth.

Danny understood. Jaywalk was here now. Jaywalk would know exactly what to do.

Jaywalk climbed out of the truck and came toward them on the run. "Are you trying to get killed today, James Allen?" he called.

"Seemed like the thing to do," Dad joked back.

90

Together they checked the "Gretchen." Salt water had gotten into the gasoline, but everything else was fine. Dad picked up his lucky hat and popped it back on his head.

"That's more like it," Jaywalk said. "Too bad the newspapers aren't here. They'd take your picture."

Dad slapped Jaywalk on the back and they walked over to Max's boat.

It was a very sad sight. The boat was all that was saved. The motor was filled with salt water. Everything else had been broken up by the strong waves or washed out to sea. Max was now a fisherman without any gear.

Max began moving toward them, his face still blank.

"What's the matter with him?" Danny whispered.

"He's in shock," Jaywalk said. "He could have drowned. He doesn't swim, you know."

Danny caught his breath. A doryman who couldn't swim? How could he go out to sea all alone? "Gee, he must have a lot of courage," Danny whispered to Dad.

Dad nodded. "Max is a strange man."

Jaywalk went to shake Max's hand. Max took it, but then he walked on toward Dad.

"I . . ." he began. "You and the boy here. . . ." He couldn't get the words out.

"Just say 'thanks,' Max," Jaywalk said. "And let it go at that."

"Thank you," Max said. Then he turned to Danny and shook his hand. "And thank you, sonny.

92

You. . . ." And then Max couldn't get the words out again. He was completely broken up.

Jaywalk put an arm around his shoulder. "Let's look at your dory, Max," he said. "I'll take your motor to my place. We'll get it all apart before the salt water ruins it."

Max nodded. So Jaywalk took over, as always. And slowly everybody got hold of themselves. The lifeguards brought them towels and they dried off a little. The men checked over Max's boat looking for damage.

Danny looked out to sea. He searched the whole blue sky. But there wasn't so much as a dot of a bird. Gink was gone. But, Danny told himself, Gink was better free than drowned. He decided that he wouldn't tell Nancy about Gink. It would only make her sad. And there was enough other stuff to talk about.

The men began loading the "Gretchen" on Jaywalk's boat trailer. They were going to take her back to the dory beach first.

"Are you okay, Danny?"

Danny turned around and it was Max. He was *smiling*. Max was really smiling. And it was very hard to believe.

"Sure, Max," Danny said. "Sure. It's just that I had to let my bird go."

"You mean one of those little gray jobs?" Max asked. "The kind that can't take off unless they are on water?"

Danny nodded.

"Well then, we'll get you another one, sonny." Max promised. "Just as soon as I go back out I'll

start looking for one. Why, I see those birds all the time."

"You do?" Danny asked. "You are?" He almost forgot Gink. He was thinking about Max going out again. Today he had almost drowned. He had lost all his gear. His boat was a mess. He still couldn't swim. But he was already planning toward the day when he would fish again.

"And I'm going to get your dad a new watch," Max said in a low voice so Dad couldn't hear. "But don't tell him. It'll be a surprise."

Suddenly Danny knew that he liked this strange, quiet man. Not the way he liked Jaywalk, maybe. But he liked Max just the same.

"Let's go," Dad called. They all got into Jaywalk's truck to pull the "Gretchen" back to the dory beach. Max waved. He was staying to guard his boat until Jaywalk came back for him.

They waved back. Danny stared back at Max. "Gosh," he finally let out a deep breath. "How come he's so nice all of a sudden?"

Jaywalk laughed out loud. "There's an old saying, Danny. 'To make a friend, first you have to be one.' "

"It's like this, Danny," Dad said slowly, staring straight ahead over the sand. "I know how Max feels. All of a sudden he isn't alone anymore."

When they reached the dory beach, Mom and Nancy rushed up to them.

"The Coast Guard told us what happened." Mom was almost in tears. "Are you both all right?" She looked from Dad to Danny.

"Fine. Just a little wet." Dad grinned. "But Max is out of business for a while."

"Let's unload the 'Gretchen' and go back for him," Jaywalk said.

"But, Dad," Danny said quickly. "Aren't we going back out for our fishing line?"

Dad gave him a tired smile. "It's too late, son. It's already noon and the other boats are in."

Danny saw that he was right. "So what are we going to do?" he asked.

"You go home with your Mom and get into dry clothes. We'll leave our line out all night and pick

97

it up early tomorrow morning."

Nancy looked worried. "Gee, Dad, we'll lose a whole day of selling."

"That's all right." Mom hugged Danny to her. "Our boys are not hurt. That's all that really matters."

Danny was glad to get home. His room looked very good to him. After a hot shower he lay down on his bed—just to rest a little, he told himself. When he woke up it was dinner time.

Dad was home and told him that they'd got Max's boat back to the dory beach. "He and Jaywalk are already at work tearing down his motor," Dad reported. "Jaywalk is going to loan Max his extra motor so he can begin fishing again."

They sat down to eat dinner. "Max is telling everybody how brave you were this morning, Danny," Dad said. "He can't get over it. He keeps saying: 'Only ten years old. Only ten years old.'"

"Danny is as smart as any kid I know," Jim said proudly.

Nancy giggled and Danny felt like taking a poke

at her. Why did girls always wreck everything? he
wondered.

"I just hope our line's okay," Danny said gruffly.

"Do you want me to come out with you tomorrow,
Dad?" Jim asked.

"No, stay with the 'Princess,' " Dad said. "Danny
and I can manage fine."

But the next morning things began to go wrong.
Getting out through those high waves was hard
enough. But when they got to their line, Dad got
mad.

"Somebody has been messing around," he said
right away.

Danny leaned over the spray rail for a better
look. The line was all twisted and snarled. Fish
were missing off the hooks.

"Some pleasure boat has just helped themselves,"
Dad snapped. "How do you like that?"

It was slow, hard work to get the line unsnarled.
What the pleasure boat hadn't taken, sharks had
eaten.

They didn't have time to troll. Helplessly they started in with their poor catch.

They got to the beach late and got last spot. Jaywalk helped push them up the beach.

"Too bad," was all he said, but his face was as angry-looking as Dad's.

"We won't make expenses today," Danny heard Dad tell Mom.

Nancy just stood around, not knowing what to do. Very few customers walked all the way down the boardwalk.

Suddenly Danny had an idea. "Say, Dad, you don't need us here. Why don't Nancy and I bait hooks today and make up for our bad day?"

Dad ruffled his hair. "You're a good boy. Go ahead, but the money is all yours. I can't pay you for yesterday or today."

"Sure, Dad." And Danny was off. He did Jaywalk's buckets of hooks first, then another doryman's baiting. By then it was late and he was hungry.

George came by. "Got a little cash?"

Danny shook his head. "We had two bad days.

104

But Mom brought down some sandwiches."

They ate up all the sandwiches. Then they sat around and talked until it was safe to take a swim.

"Hey, Nance," George called. "Want to come? Are you a strong swimmer?"

Nancy giggled. "No, but I'm pretty good in the bathtub."

Everybody laughed. Then George and Danny raced toward the waves. The high summer waves were hard on a little dory boat. But for a surfer they were the most exciting. Many more surfers were in the water, and Danny was careful not to get hit by a board. That could really hurt.

When Danny got back, Dad and Nancy were putting away all the gear.

"How'd we do?" Danny asked.

Dad smiled. "Not bad. Not bad at all."

"Jaywalk slipped us some rock cod," Nancy whispered. "Wasn't that nice of him? He didn't *have* to do that."

After the boat was cleaned up Danny went to look for Jaywalk. He found him talking to some

105

customers who were taking photographs. Tourists, probably. Mrs. Jaywalk just listened and smiled.

"He'll talk to a lamppost if there aren't any people around," she told Danny.

Danny walked up to their friend. He stuck out his hand. "I just want to say thanks."

Jaywalk smiled while the tourists watched. He knew what Danny meant, but he never let on.

"Sure thing, boy. You can bait my hooks anytime. Anytime!" Then he turned back to the eager tourists.

Danny winked at Mrs. Jaywalk and went back to the "Gretchen." "There was never anybody like Jaywalk," he thought warmly. "Nobody in this whole wide world."

The next morning they went out early. They wanted to make up for the last two bad days.

While Dad was setting the line, Danny heard the familiar sound of flapping wings.

Slap. Slap. It was Gink. He landed on their spray rail. Gink had come back.

106

"Look, Dad," he cried. "It's Gink. See the missing tail feathers? It's the same bird."

"Nutty bird," Dad said. "Now he's stuck again."

Danny grinned. "He likes us, Dad." He offered a fish scrap to Gink.

Snap. The bird gobbled it up.

"He's no fool," Dad said. "He gets free meals on this boat."

Boy, Danny thought, was it ever good to have Gink back. Maybe he was a silly-looking little bird. He didn't make a sound. But that smart look in his eyes let you know what he was thinking. Gink hopped around, jerking his head first to the right, then to the left.

"He's watching you, Dad," Danny said.

"He's a watch bird, all right. Want to keep him, Danny?"

"Sure do." He held his breath. Would Dad say yes?

"Will *you* take care of him?" Dad asked.

"Oh, sure. He won't be any trouble. He eats fish scraps. He can sleep on top of our locker."

108

"Okay," Dad was smiling. "He's a funny little fellow, but he's all yours."

"Thanks, Dad," Danny said. "Nancy and me, we'll take good care of him."

"Say, Danny"—Dad threw over the black flag marker—"do you have enough money for your bike?"

Danny blushed. He was short and there was only a week until school started. Those ten-speeders sure cost a lot of money.

He shook his head. "I guess I'll have to get some extra baiting jobs," he said slowly.

"How much are you short?" Dad asked.

"Ten dollars." Danny looked down at his hands. "Maybe . . . well, I still have a week before school starts."

"You'll make it, Danny," Dad said. "You would have made it by now if we'd gone out every day. But everybody needs a day off once a week."

Dad's words made Danny feel better. It was time to change places to begin trolling. When Danny stood up he saw something floating in the water.

"Hey, Dad, what's that?"

Dad fished it out with his gaff. It was a bundle of papers all tied together with string. That was why it had floated instead of sinking.

They looked down at the bundle. On the top in big black letters it read: TOP SECRET—BURN.

They stared at one another. "Why, these are important," Dad said in surprise. "They must have fallen off a Navy ship."

"Gee, Dad," Danny asked, "what are we going to do with them? Can we open them?"

NANCY'S DAY GETS CLOSER

Dad turned the secret papers over in his hands. "I don't know, Danny," he said. "We have no right to open secret papers."

"But, Dad, we can't just throw them back in the sea," Danny said.

"No . . . but . . ."—Dad looked up—". . . but we can take them back to the beach and call up the Coast Guard. They'll tell us what to do."

"Ah, gee. . . ." Danny was disappointed, but he understood. "Maybe they'll let us watch while *they* open them."

Danny looked around the open sea. "Isn't it exciting to find secret papers just floating around this big ocean?" He stretched his arms out wide.

Dad laughed. "More exciting than finding oranges or onions."

Danny held his nose. "Remember when some ship dumped a whole crate of onions and they washed ashore and smelled up the place for a week?"

Dad chuckled while he put the papers under the seat in a safe, dry place. "How about that time all the bamboo floated in? There were great big tree trunks?"

Danny remembered. "And the little kids were hunting for treasure," he said.

"Not just little kids," Dad reminded him. "A lot of grown-ups were hunting, too."

"But only Jaywalk found the glass float off a fishing ship," Danny said.

"It must have come off a ship from Japan," Dad

said. "They use those glass floats over there on their fishing nets."

Danny looked out to sea again. He thought about how far away Japan was. It was a long way across the ocean. But it was still close enough to float a glass ball all the way to their dory beach.

"How come Jaywalk finds so much stuff?" Danny asked.

"Because he's an efficient beachcomber," Dad chuckled. "He's got more junk in that locker of his. . . ." Dad had the trolling lines ready. "Okay Danny, let's go."

Danny cranked the motor and started toward their trolling place. Boy, did they have something to show to Jaywalk! He always said he was looking for gold and treasure. But *they* had found top-secret papers. Nobody had ever found anything like that.

While they trolled and Dad brought in fish after fish, Danny enjoyed himself. What a day! First Gink came back. Then they found the secret papers.

How neat! Jim had never found anything this exciting on board the "Princess." Why, those papers

114

might even be in code. They might tell where the Navy was going next. The Coast Guard might even call up Washington with the news. And then who could tell what might happen.

Danny wiggled out of his jacket. The sun was warm now. He shivered a little—not from the cold, but from excitement. Boy, anything could happen! He could hardly wait to get ashore.

But Dad trolled slowly for an hour. Then they went back to pull up their line. They had a good catch.

Before they started in, Danny put Gink in the bottom of the boat. He didn't want to take any chances of losing his pet again.

"Here, Gink, here's a goodie," Danny said.

The bird looked at Danny. Then he walked around the bottom of the boat. Snap. He gobbled up the fish scrap. When he looked at Danny for more, Danny laughed.

They got back to the beach in a few minutes. Mom and Nancy came down the boardwalk to meet them.

Danny waved wildly. He didn't know which to

show them first—Gink or the secret papers.

In his excitement he jumped out of the boat too soon. Splash. He was up to his neck in water.

"Take it easy, son," Dad said. "The papers will still be there when we get in."

Danny blushed. Then he swam along the side, pushing the "Gretchen" in toward shore.

"What are you doing, Danny?" Mom called. "It's too early to go swimming."

Nancy giggled behind her hand. Danny made a face. "You might know," he thought. "Girls act so silly."

But Nancy forgot to tease when she saw Gink. "Aw, how sweet," she cried. "Let me hold him! Oh, please!"

Gently Danny handed the bird to her. Gink hooked his claws around her finger and sat there, blinking in the sun. Nancy squealed with delight. "He's just wonderful," she gasped.

"What kind is he?" Mom asked with a smile.

"We don't know," Danny said. "We call him 'Gink.' "

117

"Come on, Ginky baby," Nancy said softly. She sounded as if she were talking to a baby.

"Hey, Mom, we've got something else." Danny just couldn't wait to get ashore before telling her. "We found some secret papers floating around in the sea."

Mom turned to Dad. He nodded.

They pushed the boat up onto shore. Then Dad reached under the seat and brought out the bundle of papers. Mom was just as surprised as they had been.

"What do you think they are, Jim?" she asked Dad.

"I don't know. But I'll call up the Coast Guard before we do anything."

By now all the dorymen on the beach had come down to see their catch. But as always, Jaywalk was in the lead.

"I thought you fished for fish, James Allen," he began. "I'm the junkman around here." But when he saw the bundle of papers he grew red in the face with excitement.

118

"You've got something big there," he said. "Let's call the Secretary of the Navy in Washington."

"We're not doing anything until I call in the Coast Guard," Dad said in a flat voice. And that settled the matter.

They pushed up the "Gretchen" and she took second spot. Max had the first spot. He was fishing with his own gear again and was very friendly with everybody. As Jaywalk said, "Max isn't all scrunched up inside anymore."

"Maybe you'll get a reward," Max said when he saw the papers.

Danny gasped. "Do you really think so?" Boy, that would be exciting! It might mean he'd get his ten-speeder after all.

"You set up shop," Dad said, putting the papers under his arm. "I'm going to make a telephone call." He strode up the boardwalk.

Danny and Mom worked fast to get the boat set up as the fish shop. After a minute Danny looked up.

"Hey, Mom, Nancy is goofing off," he said.

Sure enough. Nancy was walking around with Gink on her finger, showing him off.

"Nancy!" Mom's voice made her jump. "You have chores."

Nancy came right over, but she pushed into Danny. "That's for telling," she whispered.

"Goof-off," Danny whispered back.

"Am not."

"Are, too!"

"Children!" Mom was angry now. "If you don't stop, the bird goes back to sea."

They worked together and didn't say anything. Danny was too excited to stay mad.

When the fish shop was set up, Danny began cleaning fish while Nancy washed them. Gink sat up on top of the weighing scales. A few customers stopped just to look at him—and bought fish.

Mom smiled. "That silly bird is good for business," she said.

"He's our good luck charm," Danny said.

"School starts in a week," Nancy said in a low voice.

122

"I know it." He went on cleaning.

"Well, I get to go out with you the last day, re-member?" She was getting sassy again and Danny didn't like it.

"I know. You don't have to brag."

"You're so smart because you go out every day." Nancy was really acting up.

Danny looked up at Mom, but she hadn't heard. He jabbed at Nancy with his elbow to keep her quiet. She jabbed back at him. There was going to be a fight. . . .

But Dad came back and stopped everything. "The Coast Guard is coming right over," he said. "When they get here, send them to the coffee shop. I've got to drink something hot. I think I took a chill."

"Oh, dear," Mom said. "I hope not."

Dad shrugged and went back up the boardwalk, holding tight to the secret papers.

Later, two officers in sharp Coast Guard uniforms arrived. Danny ran to get Dad from the coffee shop. They all hurried back to the "Gretchen."

The Captain looked at the papers. "I never saw

anything like this before," he said slowly. "We'll have to burn them, just like it says."

Ed, Jaywalk, and all the dorymen and their wives crowded around.

"Can't we take a little look inside?" Jaywalk asked with a big smile.

The Captain frowned in thought.

"He can charm the scales off a fish," Mrs. Jaywalk whispered.

Danny and Nancy laughed.

"All right," the Captain finally said. "Anybody got a knife?"

Danny handed him their sharpest cleaning knife.

The Captain put the papers down on their cutting board and cut the string. He looked through the papers for a minute. Everybody leaned forward eagerly.

He looked up. "Sorry to disappoint you folks. It's just a bunch of shipping orders."

Everybody sighed and groaned. Then they began to go back to their own boats.

"You sure there's nothing else?" Jaywalk pressed

closer. "Something you overlooked?"

The Captain frowned and gave Jaywalk a funny look.

Jaywalk stepped back. "Sorry, it's just the beach-comber in me."

"Maybe it's a joke," Dad said.

"Maybe," said the Captain. "But we can't take chances. Anybody got a match? We'll burn these in a fire circle."

"Can I help?" Danny asked. "I found the papers."

"Okay, kid." They walked over to the fire circle. The sight of the uniforms brought all the surfers in from the sea.

"Hi, sport," George said. "What gives?"

Quickly Danny told him.

George whistled. "Man, what a blast!" he said.

The Captain opened the bundle and struck a match. Then they all stood watching. Soon the last paper was burned.

They walked back to the dory beach. "Thanks for calling us, Mr. Allen," the Captain said to Dad. "You did the right thing."

128

Dad nodded and they shook hands. Danny was disappointed. No paper in code. No Navy secrets. And no reward. But he still had Gink and a good fish catch to sell. He felt a hand on his shoulder.

It was Dad. "Listen, son, will you take over for me?" Dad asked. "I'm going home."

"Sure, Dad," Danny said. "What's the matter?"

"I don't know." Dad's face was white-looking. "I don't feel well." He turned and walked up the boardwalk slowly—not like Dad usually walked up the boardwalk.

Danny went back to the cutting board. He knew that Mom was worried, but she didn't say anything. Nancy had settled down. They worked the rest of the morning and far into the afternoon.

When they got home that night, Dad was in bed. He was very ill.

They didn't take the "Gretchen" out the next day. Or the next. Mom stayed home, too. But Nancy and Danny just stood around the dory beach. They played with Gink. They helped push up the dory boats.

129

"There's nothing to do," Nancy finally said. "Maybe I won't get out with you."

"Then let's bait hooks," Danny told her. "I've got to earn another ten dollars to buy my bike."

"What if you don't make it?" Nancy asked. "School starts in three days."

"I've got to," Danny said. "I have this dream . . . I want to ride my bike to school the very first day."

"Listen," Nancy said quickly. "You bait Max's hooks and I'll bait Jaywalk's. That'll give you two more dollars."

Danny was stunned. "You mean that you'd give me your money?" he asked.

Nancy grinned shyly. "Well, you gave me Gink, didn't you?"

Danny felt like hugging her. But he didn't.

"Okay," he said. "Let's go to work."

LOST AT SEA

It was the day before school started. Danny stood on the beach and watched the gulls making circles in the air. They yelled for food in loud voices. They stole food from one another in midair. Those old gulls never stopped, Danny thought.

He walked back up the boardwalk to help Dad. They were going out today. It was Dad's first day out of bed. Mom didn't like it one bit. But Dad had

131

promised Nancy. Besides, they needed a good fishing day to make up for the time lost when Dad had been sick.

Jim had wanted to take out the "Gretchen" this morning. But Dad had sent him off to work on the "Princess."

"Danny and I can manage," Dad had said.

Danny looked around the empty beach. "Where's Jaywalk?" he asked.

"He's gone," Dad muttered. "Everybody's gone, I guess. We must be late."

"What can I do, Daddy?" Nancy asked, her eyes very big. She hugged her arms against her chest. Danny knew it was from excitement as well as the early morning cold. He well remembered shivering in the beginning of summer. Now he was used to going out in the boat. He didn't even carry a lemon anymore.

And yet today felt different. The fog was thick. The air was heavy. It just wasn't a good day at all.

"Say, Dad, there's a creepy feeling around," Danny said.

132

"It'll blow over," Dad said, carrying the motor.

He stumbled a little as if the motor was too heavy.

Danny helped clamp the motor over the stern. He could tell Dad was still weak. If only Jaywalk could fish near them. . . .

They started to push the "Gretchen" down the boardwalk.

"Come on, Gink." Danny put the bird in the boat. "You're my good-luck bird."

Gink just looked at Danny and blinked his little black eyes.

The water was easy to cross this morning. The stillness was what was wrong. It was like . . . Danny thought slowly . . . it was like something was going to happen. The sea was too calm and too quiet. Danny couldn't smell salt or wet sand. The air was dull. But the sea never stayed that way.

"Where are we going, Dad?" Danny asked as Dad started to row. Nancy sat in the bow seat, all hunched down out of the wind.

"The red hole," Dad said.

Danny was surprised. Dad had always said that

134

the red hole was for dreamers.

"Where's that?" Nancy asked.

"About six miles out from the pier," Danny explained. "If everything is just right—the tide, the current, and the wind—we'll get a fish on every hook."

"And what if everything isn't just right?" Nancy asked.

"We'll pull up an almost empty line," Danny told her.

"That's right," Dad muttered. "It's the chance we take—all or nothing."

Danny looked at Dad in surprise. Even his voice sounded funny.

He looked over at Nancy. He smiled and winked. He didn't want her to know that he was worried. She smiled back at him excitedly.

Dad rowed through the first gentle waves. Then he cranked the motor and they shot out to sea. Dad lined up the compass with the red hole. They rode in a straight line for six miles. The fog closed around them. All they could see was a few feet ahead of the

136

boat. Danny watched for floating logs so he could tell Dad to turn fast.

"Good old Gink." Danny stroked down the bird's feathers. Gink moved along the spray rail near Danny. "Gink will bring us luck," Danny thought. "I just know he will."

Dad cut the motor and the boat drifted. They were at the red hole. Danny looked around. It didn't look any different than the rest of the sea. But the dorymen had been fishing this spot for years.

"Pull the bait bucket up here, Danny," Dad said. "And Nancy, please move to the stern."

Danny stood up and tugged the big wooden bucket toward Dad. But it was crowded in the boat with another person. He had to half lift the tub. Dad reached for it but it slipped.

Crash. Danny froze when he heard glass breaking. The tub had smashed the compass.

"Darn it," Dad said, looking down sadly at the ruined compass. "It'll never work again."

"What'll we do now?" Danny asked over a lump in his throat.

137

"Listen for the foghorns," Dad said. Both jetties on shore had foghorns. One had a high sound and the other a deep sound. "If we steer between the two sounds we'll hit the dory beach."

Danny let out a deep breath. Maybe it wasn't so bad after all, he told himself.

Dad set the line and put an extra black marker on the float. That way they could find their line in the thick fog.

"We hit the red hole," Dad said. "Now it'll work for us."

"Gee, Daddy, you did that fast." Nancy was seeing everything for the first time. And she was full of wonder. She moved up front again.

Dad nodded and baited the trolling lines. Danny ran the motor, and right away Dad had a strike. Quickly he stood up to pull in the big bonito. But he fell sideways and had to catch himself.

"What's the matter, Dad?" Danny asked.

Dad looked dazed. "Don't know. Got dizzy, I guess," he murmured.

Danny looked at Nancy. All of a sudden she

looked scared stiff and very little.

Next time Dad got a strike he stood up again. When he lost his balance Danny reached out to save him. But Dad fell over and hit his head on the wooden bucket. Then he just lay still.

"Dad!" Danny yelled, cutting the motor.

"Daddy!" Nancy cried out.

They both reached him at the same time. They rolled him over.

"He doesn't look too hurt," Danny said.

"But his face is so white," Nancy cried. "Oh, Danny, he won't wake up! Is he dead?"

Danny sprinkled a few drops of water on Dad's face. He didn't move. But then Danny saw that he was still breathing.

"He's just passed out, Nancy." He tried to keep his voice steady. "That hit on his head must have been pretty rough."

Danny looked up and around. He saw nothing but gray fog. The whitecaps were breaking up to the spray railing. He knew that the small-craft warnings must be up on shore. That meant that the sea

141

was too dangerous for a small boat. But they were six miles out—alone and helpless.

He looked at Nancy and didn't know what to say. She looked very scared, but she didn't say anything. She just put Dad's head on her lap and stroked his cheek.

"I'll get us in," Danny said. He stood up. Dad had said they should listen for the foghorns. But . . . Danny waited, listening hard. He couldn't hear anything, anything at all. The thick fog was dulling the sound of the foghorns.

Okay, he thought quickly. The compass was smashed. The fog was so thick he couldn't hear the foghorns. Now what?

"Hey, Gink," Danny scooped up his bird. "You know the way back to shore. Take off, Gink. And we'll follow you."

He put the bird down into the choppy sea. Gink beat his wings wildly. Then he took off.

"Quick, keep Dad comfortable," Danny said. He cranked the motor for all he was worth. It started, but when he looked for Gink, the bird had gone off

144

into the fog. Everywhere Danny looked it was the same—the gray fog and the choppy sea.

"Gink! Hey, Gink," Danny called.

There was no sound, no sound at all.

"We're lost, aren't we, Danny?" Nancy's voice was very small. "We're lost at sea!"

Danny slumped down into his seat. The waves were now washing into the boat. They had to get going. But which way? He stared around wildly. Which way was the shore? Nancy didn't know anything about the sea. It was all up to him.

"Don't worry, Nance," he said. "We'll find the dory beach." But he didn't look at her when he said it.

He cranked the motor and steered blindly in one direction. All he found was more sea, wind, and fog. He stopped again. This way he was just wasting gasoline.

Danny sat very still, his mind going around and around. Gink was gone. They were alone and helpless. Nobody could find them way out here. And if Nancy started to cry. . . .

But she didn't. She sat there quietly and let him think. And, boy oh boy, did he ever need to think.

Danny stared down at the rough water for a long time. He had to fight back the tears. If he got silly and cried, well, then he never could save them, could he?

He looked down at Dad. He was gray looking, but still breathing. At least he hadn't been killed in that fall. But Dad needed a doctor right away. And their dory beach was just a few minutes away. *But which way?*

Lost at Sea

Danny thought about old Jaywalk's words. "You always keep an eye on Mother Sea. She can turn on you quick as a minute."

Jaywalk was sure right about that. He was right about a lot of things. Funny, silly things like the swells always coming from the same direction. . . .

Danny sat up straight, his eyes wide open. That was it! That would get them back to shore.

He said out loud, "Jaywalk told me that the swells always come from the same direction, from the southwest, unless. . . ."

Nancy leaned forward. "Unless what?"

Danny closed his eyes and tried to remember. ". . . unless the wind is from the southeast," he said excitedly. "That will turn the swell."

"How was the wind this morning?" Nancy asked in a tiny voice.

"It was from the southwest," Danny said quickly. "And I don't think it has changed. Anyway, Nance, we have to try. We just *have* to."

"Wait until I make Daddy comfortable," Nancy said in a tight, scared voice. "Okay, let's go."

With his heart beating somewhere around his throat, Danny cranked the motor. He steered the dory boat at a forty-five degree angle across the swells. He didn't go too fast for fear of hitting a log or something.

Five minutes went by. Ten. Fifteen. "Maybe I was wrong," he thought shakily. "Maybe Jaywalk said something else. Maybe. . . ."

"Danny," Nancy cried out. "I see the pier."

Danny stared. Sure enough. The pilings of the pier stood out from the fog. They'd made it! Just

148

around the pier was the dory beach. Danny yelled for joy. "Hooo-ray!"

Now Nancy was crying and laughing at the same time. And Danny felt as if he was on air instead of rough water.

"Here we go!" He shot up the motor to full speed and ran the boat in to shore. As the boat hit soft sand, Jaywalk grabbed the railing.

"My sakes, boy," Jaywalk said thickly. "I didn't know if you could make it there for a minute." Then he saw Dad.

"What happened?" he demanded.

Danny jumped out and explained. Jaywalk sent Ed running for a doctor. Mom came down to meet them. Her face turned as white as Dad's.

Somehow they got the "Gretchen" and Dad up on shore. All the dorymen gathered around. Everybody talked at once.

Ed brought the doctor who looked Dad over. Danny held his breath. They all waited.

"The bump on his head isn't bad," the doctor finally said. "What made him pass out?"

150

"He's been very sick," Mom said. "He must have been weak."

The doctor nodded. "Well, just put him to bed for a good rest."

Dad woke up. "What happened?" he asked thickly.

Danny started to explain. "Well, we—"

But Nancy broke in. "Oh, Danny was so wonderful. The compass was broken and Gink flew away. I was ready to cry, but Danny, he remembered about the swells coming from the southwest. . . ."

Jim came running and heard what Nancy said. "Good for you, Danny," he said.

"Oh, *Danny!*" Mom hugged him in front of everybody. "That was very smart of you."

"I always knew you were a good kid." Max ruffled his hair.

Danny turned red as a beet. He didn't know what to say. "It was really nothing," he said.

"That's my boy," Dad said, as Jaywalk and Ed helped him to their truck. "I've got me two fisherman sons. How can I miss?"

The dorymen laughed and went back to their own boats. Jaywalk looked out toward sea. "I'll go pick up your line after the fog lifts," he said.

"Thanks, Jaywalk," Dad said.

"Hey, Gink." Danny saw his pet bird waddling around. "You flew too fast for me to follow. But you did come back and wait for us."

Jim looked at Danny in surprise. "Gee, Dan, that was smart to try the bird. And I didn't know the swells had any direction," Jim said. "I guess it pays to listen to old Jaywalk."

"It sure does," Danny agreed.

They started up the boardwalk toward the pick-up truck.

"Hey, Dan," Jim said suddenly. "There is no business here today. Let's go pick out that ten-speeder of yours."

Danny shook his head. "I don't have enough money," he said sadly. "I saved up all summer, but I'm still five dollars short."

"I have a dollar I can loan you," Nancy said quickly.

154

"You don't have to," Jim said excitedly. "I've got news for you, Danny. The bike shop is having a sale. That good ten-speed bike is marked down ten dollars."

Danny stared at him for a minute. He had to be sure Jim wasn't kidding.

He wasn't kidding! Danny let out a yell. "Yippee! Let's go and ask Mom if she needs us."

"You go ahead," Mom said. "I'll just take Dad home and put him to bed."

Jim and Danny started off.

"Hey, wait for me," Nancy called.

Jim and Danny turned and waved. They didn't mind if she tagged along. Suddenly Danny had an idea.

"Hey, Nance. I'll buy you that new doll with my leftover money."

Nancy stopped short. "You will?" she cried. Then she began to jump up and down. "Oh, Danny, you are the best brother!"

The three of them started off. Danny didn't mind being in the middle anymore. His big brother was

155

great, as always. Even that little sister of his wasn't so bad, either.

"Come on, Gink," Danny called to his bird.

"Hey," Jaywalk called from the truck. "You kids can't take a seabird into a bike shop."

Danny laughed out loud. "Want to bet?" he called back. "Gink is going to ride on my handle-bars!"

Whitman TWEEN-AGE BOOKS

**IN-BETWEEN BOOKS FOR
IN-BETWEEN READERS**

**Walt Disney's DONALD DUCK
AND THE LOST MESA RANCH** Mary Carey

DORY BOY Joan Talmage Weiss

HERE, BOY! Lots of Stories for Everyone Who Likes Dogs

THAT'S OUR CLEO! And Other Stories About Cats

Not too easy, not too hard, just lots of fun!

ABOUT THE AUTHOR

Writer Joan Talmage Weiss spends summers at Newport Beach, California. "The dory beach is a most remarkable place," she says, "the only dory fishing fleet left on this coast. From my first visit to the dory fleet I knew there was a book there." Indeed there was! The book became DORY BOY, in which Mrs. Weiss tells the story of Danny whose family's livelihood depends upon the sea.

Joan Weiss approaches her writing of children's books with a sure hand. She has been writing since childhood and has a keen recollection of things she particularly liked to read. She finds, too, that her three children Kenny, Lorraine, and Nancy are helpful. They provide not only a ready reading audience, but insight into the tastes of today's children.

DORY BOY is Mrs. Weiss's second book for Whitman. Her earlier book, KENNY AND HIS ANIMAL FRIENDS, took a first award for juvenile fiction in state-wide California Press Women competition and later won first place honors in the National Press Women competition.